Pip and Posy

www.worldofpipandposy.com

For Enzo
A.S.

First published 2012 by Nosy Crow Ltd
The Crow's Nest, 10a Lant Street
London SE1 1QR
www.nosycrow.com

This edition first published 2014

ISBN 978 0 85763 296 8

A CIP catalogue record for this book is available from the British Library.

Printed in Turkey by Imago

Papers used by Nosy Crow are made from wood grown
in sustainable forests.

7 9 8 6

Pip and Posy
The Snowy Day

Axel Scheffler

nosy crow

It was a very snowy day.
Pip and Posy wanted
to go out and play.

So they
put on their
warm jumpers . . .

their stripy socks . . .

their puffy coats . . .

. . . their waterproof boots,
their cosy scarves
and their woollen mittens.

Then they went out
into the snow.

Wherever they walked,
they left big footprints.

They caught snowflakes on
their tongues.

They even made snow angels
with big wings. It was such good fun.

Next, they pulled their sledge
up to the top of the hill . . .

. . . and zoomed down the other side.

"WHEEE!" they shouted.

Then Posy had an idea.
"Let's build a snowmouse!" she said.

"But I want a snow rabbit!" said Pip.

"Snow**mouse**,"
said Posy.

"Snow**RABBIT**," said Pip.

Posy was so cross with Pip that she threw the snowmouse's head at him.

Oh dear!

Then Pip was so cross with Posy
that he pushed her very hard
and she fell into the snow.

Oh dear!

Now Pip and Posy
were **very** cold
and **very** sad indeed.

Poor Pip! Poor Posy!

Then Posy did a very kind thing.

"I am sorry for making you
all snowy, Pip," she said.

"And I am sorry for pushing you," said Pip.

They decided to go inside again, where it was nice and warm.

They took off all their wet things.

And then they got out their playdough
and made mice AND rabbits.

And frogs and pigs and birds, and elephants and cows and giraffes, as well!

Hooray!